More BUNNY TROUBLE

ISBN 0-590-41590-5

Copyright © 1989 by Hans Wilhelm Inc.
All rights reserved. Published by Scholastic Inc.

12 11 10 9 8 7 6 5 4 3 2 1   3   0 1 2 3 4 5/9

Printed in the U.S.A.   23

More BUNNY TROUBLE

by Hans Wilhelm

SCHOLASTIC INC.
New York Toronto London Auckland Sydney

On the day before Easter, Ralph was out
kicking his soccer ball—just what he liked to
do most.

Then his mother told him to watch his
little sister Emily—just what he didn't like to
do most.

He couldn't understand why his mother
and father made such a fuss about Emily.
She cried a lot and was always wet.

Ralph thought Emily must be the noisiest,
messiest baby in the whole world.

Ralph's mother gave him some Easter eggs to decorate and a blanket to sit on.

"Be sure that your sister does not crawl into the tall grass," she told Ralph.

Ralph was trying to concentrate on his painting when Emily reached over to touch the eggs.

"Stop that!" Ralph said, and he poked her with his paw. Not too hard, but not too gently, either—just enough to make Emily cry.

Mama came running. "What's the matter with Emily?" she asked Ralph.

"I don't know," Ralph said, pretending to be busy painting an egg.

But Ralph's mother had a good idea of what had happened. "Ralph, I have told you over and over again— paws are not made for hitting."

Ralph bowed his head. "Yes, mama," he said.

But as soon as their mother was back inside, Ralph poked his little sister again.

Emily cried and cried. But this time her mother did not come. Instead two butterflies flew by and fluttered around Emily's head.

She quickly forgot about the hurt and started after the pretty blue creatures.

Emily crawled off the
blanket and headed straight for
the tall green grass.

It was a whole new world
for Emily, filled with animals
and flowers she had never seen
before.

Everything was so pretty and
smelled so good. Emily looked
around, and then she went on
crawling. On and on....

Suddenly Ralph looked up and saw that his sister was gone!

"Oh, no!" he cried. "I was supposed to be watching her. Where did she go? How did she get away so fast?"

"EMILY!" he called as loudly as he could. "E-M-I-L-Y!" But there was no answer.

Ralph looked
everywhere. He listened,
trying to hear his sister's
cry. Nothing.

"Oh, dear! She must have
gone into the tall grass!
Anything could happen in
there. A fox could get her,
or an eagle, or a snake...I
have to find her!"

But the grass was so tall Ralph could not see anything.

He ran to his mother and told her the whole story.

Ralph's mother did not lose any time. She called the neighbors together and asked them to help her find the baby.

All the rabbits were busy getting eggs ready for Easter. But this was more important. They stopped their work and ran out into the tall grass.

Each rabbit set off in a different direction. The field was so large and there were so few rabbits—how could they possibly search every spot? Besides, in the thick grass, they could easily pass right by the baby without even seeing her.

"Emily! Emily!" they cried.

Still no answer.

Where was Emily? Could she hear them?

Someone did hear the rabbits calling. It was a fox!
He knew immediately what had happened.

He licked his chops. "With a little bit of luck, I'll have myself a delicious baby rabbit for supper!" he said.

And with that, the fox joined the search for little Emily.

Emily's mother was getting frantic. "It's late," she cried. "We have to find Emily before the sun goes down."

"We need more help," said one of the neighbors. "The grass is so thick and tall and there are so few of us."

Then Ralph spoke up. "I know what we can do! Listen, everybody. I think I have the answer."

The rabbits stopped their search and gathered around Ralph.

"Here is my idea," Ralph said. "We will all hold paws together and walk in a long line across the field. That way we can cover every inch. We can't miss her."

All the rabbits thought this was a good idea. They joined paws and combed through the tall grass.

And that's how they found
little Emily, fast asleep, dreaming
of butterflies.